for **Nelson**
(good boy)

Text and illustrations © 2008 Mo Willems

First Edition, April 2008

11 12 13 14 15 16 17 18 19 20

FAC-029191-18200

Printed in Malaysia

Reinforced binding

This book is hand-lettered by Mo Willems, with additional text set in Helvetica Neue LT Pro and Latino Rumba/Monotype.

ISBN-13: 978-1-4231-0960-0
ISBN-10: 1-4231-0960-0

Library of Congress Cataloging-in-Publication Data on file.

Visit www.hyperionbooksforchildren.com
and www.pigeonpresents.com

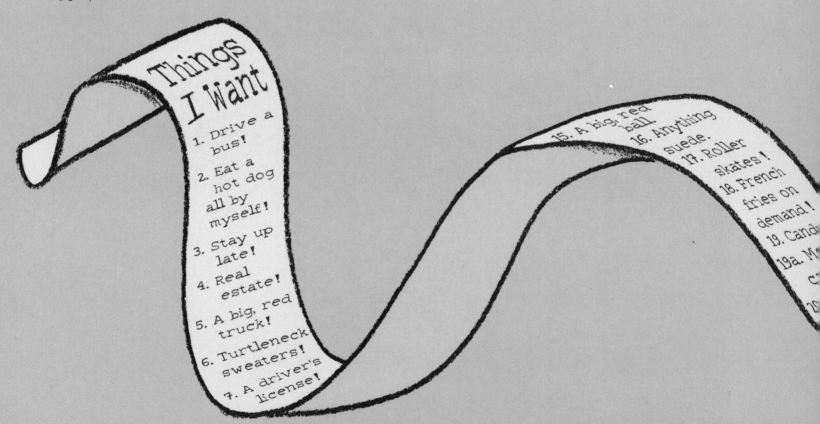

Things I Want

1. Drive a bus!
2. Eat a hot dog all by myself!
3. Stay up late!
4. Real estate!
5. A big, red truck!
6. Turtleneck sweaters!
7. A driver's license!

15. A big, red ball.
16. Anything suede.
17. Roller skates!
18. French fries on demand!
19. Cand
19a. M

The Pigeon Wants a Puppy!

words and pictures by mo willems

Hyperion Books for Children
New York
An Imprint of Disney Book Group

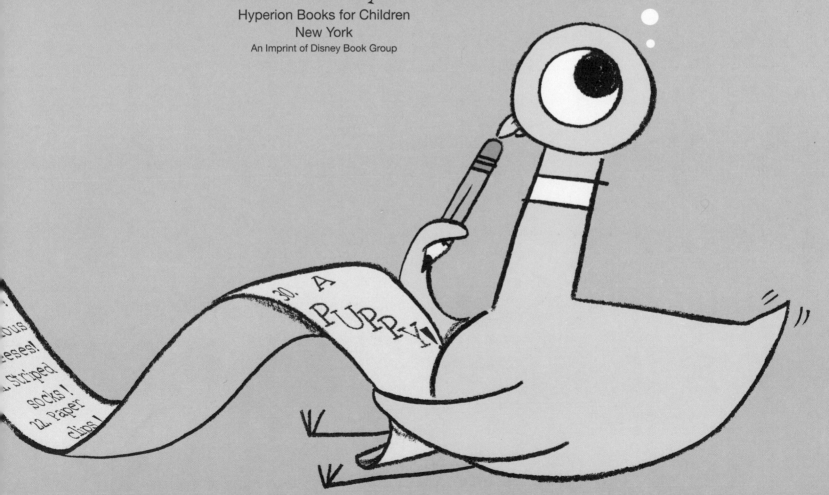

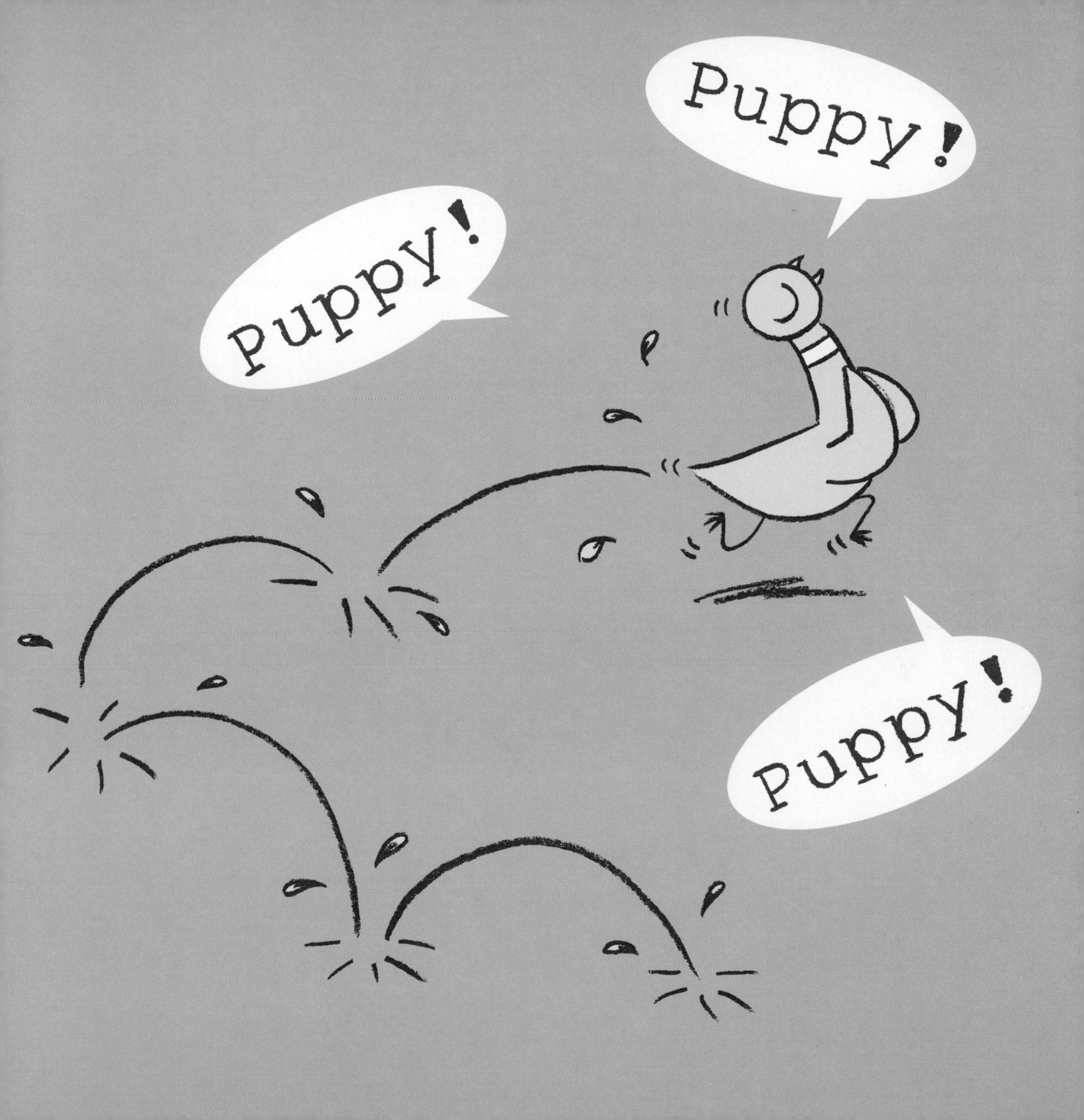
Puppy!
Puppy!
Puppy!

I WANT A PUPPY! RIGHT HERE! RIGHT NOW!

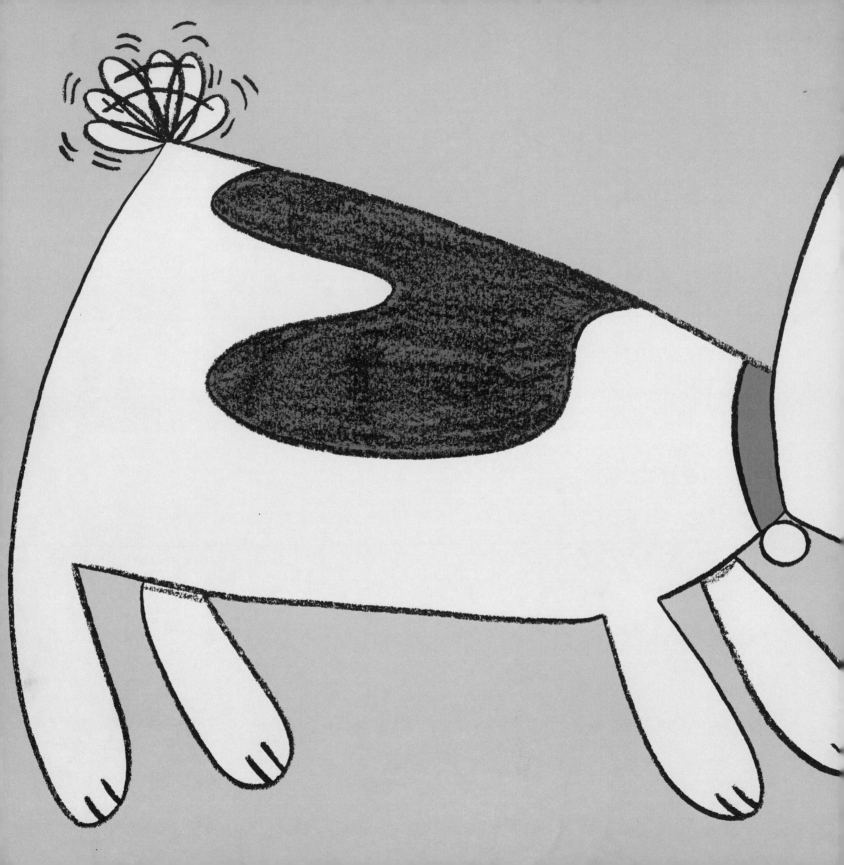